"Just as the waters of Lake Michigan and Lake Huron meet, making them, in some ways, a single lake, so too do the voices of Linda Nemec Foster and Anne-Marie Oomen converge in their new collaboration, and so too do the voices and lives of their principal characters. In this tale, much is intertwined: image and text, the lives of sisters, and mystery and maturity. In this way, a story of a mermaid and a young woman serves as a reminder that all of our lives are and should be inexorably connected to our Great Lakes."

—Cindy Hunter Morgan, author of *Harborless* and *Far Company* (both Wayne State University Press)

"*The Lake Huron Mermaid* is a beautiful book in both text and image. Dawn longs for her sister's return home and return to health. In her struggle, she turns to nearby Lake Huron 'as though / the lakes, too, were *sistered*.' In the fluid drawings and flow of the narrative, the lakes Huron and Michigan indeed are sisters who meet at Mackinac. Science and myth, logic and intuition, also emerge as sisters. To convey in formal poetic terms the relationship between these multiple pairs of sisters, the choice of a sonnet with its octave and sestet is perfect. In 'The Long Journey Back,' the two sonnet stanzas are sisters that affirm the close relation between the other pairs of sisters: Dawn and Kate, Huron and Michigan, science and myth. They are all 'Bound to each other, closer now: like the shore to the water's edge.'"

—Margaret Rozga, 2019–20 Wisconsin Poet Laureate and author of *Restoring Prairie* and *Holding My Selves Together: New and Selected Poems*

"Literary magicians Linda Nemec Foster and Anne-Marie Oomen, along with gifted illustrator Meridith Ridl, have made a beautiful book of poems about deep water—the literal and the metaphorical kind. Readers of all ages will dive deep then resurface, buoyed by invaluable wisdom and knowledge. This book isn't just wildly and satisfyingly imaginative; it is a genuine teaching text: about Lake Huron, about medical science, about sisterly love, and about the power of joining feeling with knowing."

—Alison Swan, author of *A Fine Canopy* (Wayne State University Press) and *Fresh Water*

"*The Lake Huron Mermaid* continues the mix of fairy tale, modern story, magic, and family that characterized its sister book, *The Lake Michigan Mermaid*. In a time of frightening pandemic, isolation, and heartache, who doesn't wish for a magic amulet, a loving sister, and a mermaid to watch over us? Sometimes fairy tales are the best reminder of what we already have, if we only look deeply enough."

—Teresa Scollon, National Endowment for the Arts fellow and author of *Trees and Other Creatures*

The
Lake Huron
Mermaid

Made in Michigan Writers Series

GENERAL EDITORS

Michael Delp, Interlochen Center for the Arts
M. L. Liebler, Wayne State University

*A complete listing of the books in this series can
be found online at wsupress.wayne.edu.*

MORE BOOKS WITH LINDA NEMEC FOSTER
AND ANNE-MARIE OOMEN

The Lake Michigan Mermaid: A Tale in Poems
Anne-Marie Oomen and Linda Nemec Foster
Illustrated by Meridith Ridl

Elemental: A Collection of Michigan Creative Nonfiction
Edited by Anne-Marie Oomen

Ghost Writers: Us Haunting Them,
Contemporary Michigan Literature
Edited by Keith Taylor and Laura Kasischke
Contribution by Anne-Marie Oomen

Abandon Automobile: Detroit City Poetry 2001
Edited by Melba Joyce Boyd and M. L. Liebler
Contribution by Linda Nemec Foster

New Poems from the Third Coast:
Contemporary Michigan Poetry
Edited by Conrad Hilberry,
Josie Kearns, and Michael Delp
Contributions by Linda Nemec Foster and
Anne-Marie Oomen

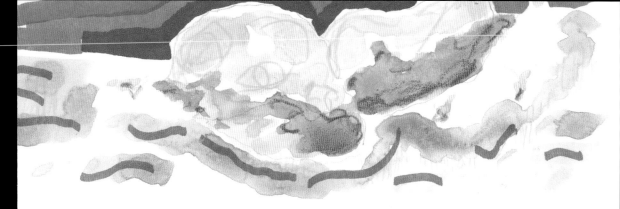

The Lake
Huron Mermaid

a tale in poems

Linda Nemec Foster
and **Anne-Marie Oomen**

Illustrated by Meridith Ridl

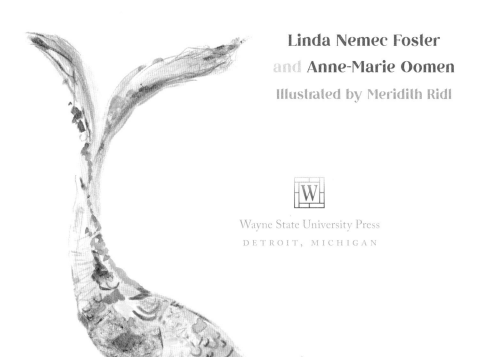

W

Wayne State University Press

DETROIT, MICHIGAN

ISBN 9780814347416 (hardcover)
ISBN 9780814347423 (e-book)

Library of Congress Control Number: 2024931668

Cover illustration by Meridith Ridl.
Cover and interior design by Lindsey Cleworth.

Publication of this book was made possible by a generous gift from The Meijer Foundation.

Wayne State University Press rests on Waawiyaataanong, also referred to as Detroit, the ancestral and contemporary homeland of the Three Fires Confederacy. These sovereign lands were granted by the Ojibwe, Odawa, Potawatomi, and Wyandot Nations, in 1807, through the Treaty of Detroit. Wayne State University Press affirms Indigenous sovereignty and honors all tribes with a connection to Detroit. With our Native neighbors, the press works to advance educational equity and promote a better future for the earth and all people.

Wayne State University Press
Leonard N. Simons Building
4809 Woodward Avenue
Detroit, Michigan 48201–1309

Visit us online at wsupress.wayne.edu.

To my one and only sister, Deborah Marie Nemec. My Debi. My dearest sister . . .
who knows so much about the secrets and longings we both share.
Love always. —LNF

To the people of FLOW (www.forloveofwater.org), water defenders led by
the intrepid Liz Kirkwood and Jim Olson, and to all my water-loving sisters
who are spirit mermaids and defenders of the Great Lakes. —AMO

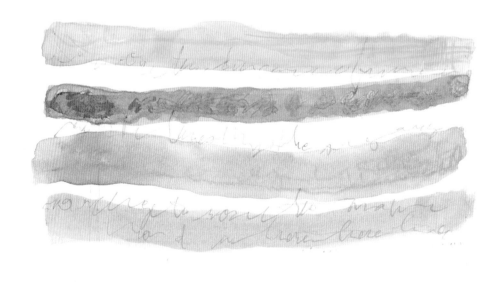

Authors' Preface

After the surprise success of *The Lake Michigan Mermaid* (thank you, readers!), we very much wanted to continue with the series and our collaboration. Wayne State University Press welcomed our proposal for more Great Lakes mermaid tales, and we set about creating *The Lake Huron Mermaid* with the support of illustrator Meridith Ridl. After a couple of bumpy starts on the manuscript, the pandemic hit, and like many writers, we shifted gears. Where we landed: this mermaid tale would continue with the themes of family and youth encountering crisis, but we also felt compelled to address what happened to families in this new world of the pandemic.

As we grappled with our own families' experiences of COVID-19, we imagined the lives of two sisters facing similar challenges. Dawn is younger and inexperienced, at an age when reality and knowledge meet belief and mystery. Kate is older, working in the medical profession, trained in science. What if Dawn, in that vulnerable stage of adolescence, encounters what so many young people encountered during the pandemic: the abrupt and harsh trauma of a beloved one's struggle with Covid? What happens if Kate survives Covid but is forever changed? And in a world where so much is fraught, what if Dawn, an athletic swimmer and diver, meets the spirit of Huron, a mermaid rising from the depths of time, from the sinkholes of the lake that may have actually changed the atmosphere of the planet eons ago?

In addition, our continued study of mermaid literature taught us that mermaid stories are rich with metaphor for the present. The mermaid does not follow the rules of logical understanding; she knows things, connects with the natural world (for example, the rising and setting of the sun) on a visceral level, senses feelings between humans, experiences parallel longings—but most of all, she possesses her own sense of wisdom, beyond human understanding. The Lake Michigan mermaid is not myth but mystery itself. And her sister, the Lake Huron mermaid, is drawn in the same way. Thus, they are a beautiful counterbalance to science.

Through the pandemic, as science worked in real time before our eyes, we realized we could not avoid that hot topic—the vaccine itself—in the imagined lives of our heroes. As Dawn grapples with the reality and uncertainty of her life, the Lake Huron mermaid faces her own uncertain longing for a distant sister. This leads to both Dawn and the mermaid needing to do the hard work of emotionally connecting with a sister—one sister changed, one long unseen. Can they do it? Is there a bridge, literal and figurative, that Dawn and the Huron mermaid can cross to save their connections to their loved ones?

Like *The Lake Michigan Mermaid*, read these poems as alternating voices—the mermaid, who is the spirit of Lake Huron, and Dawn, a girl learning to grow up. To clarify the narrators of the alternating poems, please note that the titles of the mermaid's poems are set in blue italics and the titles of Dawn's poems are in orange roman. In the last poem, "Contrapuntal: The Gift," both kinds of fonts are used since the poem is a melding of the two voices—the mermaid's and the girl's—in celebration of their friendship.

As always, we are forever grateful to readers and librarians who love poetry, who are fans of mermaids and all things mythical, and who just might be as fascinated as we were by the science of the lake's underwater world.

With love for the Great Lakes and sisters of all sorts,
Linda Nemec Foster and Anne-Marie Oomen

Morning on the Lake

Alone in my lake, I live
under the waves—those dark-blue
rolling currents. I swim
only at dawn, when the water's awakening
rhythms echo my own heart.
As I plunge down to the depths of
each dark shipwreck, as I rise to the
lake's glittering and jeweled surface,
every movement reflects a dance.
Like sunlight and shadow, like calm
and storm. But I see another dance: a woman and girl
cry and embrace on the shore.
I cannot hear their words—only witness their tears
as the waves call my name, Auroraelelacia: morning on the lake.

Dawn

We say goodbye on the beach at dawn
with about a kajillion rocks all around us.
Small joke. *Just until the curve flattens,*
she says, dressed in her scrubs, already

ready. *What if you never . . .* I can't help it—
my face is wet. She touches her finger
to my lips, smiles her lie. She says,
Stay with Aunt Claire. Keep your distance.

Wear your mask. You'll be safe.
Sure Sis, while you wear
the same mask for a whole day,
while you stand next to the wheezing?

Stay safe? Where few see me, mask or not,
where no one can touch me, virus or not,
where the town is so small it can't fix
the cracked junior high pool, and besides

they all swim in this lake, Huron,
all times of year. How's that for crazy?
So, sister, back atcha. And don't say
my name that way, like it might be

the last time I hear it in your voice
that always insists I should believe
in morning, all that light and nice,
no matter what? *Dawn*, she says again,

as if the word meant love. She hands me
her opal amulet. *It's got superpowers.* Really?
She grins. Then she's in her truck and gone,
and I'm alone, standing on the rocks.

Mystery

Before the mystery on the shore,
I had my own mystery—a forgotten song
only the deep waters sing.

A song that mirrors the life of this lake
that was birthed in glacial ice, jagged
lines of white crystals, ravines of earth displaced.

My mystery evolved from colors
that changed from rose dawn to gray dusk,
from transparent green to opaque mist.

I began my life as diffracted light—
a prism that reflected my home, Huron.
Colors of water, of ice, of sky, of light.

As if sunrise and moonrise
were created in my every turning.

And they were. The sun's length of days,
the moon's length of nights helped form
my secret, my hiding place—

the sinkhole in the lake's floor.
It glows purple and pink
like a carpet of prisms reflecting

the dawn. Imagine those colors
of morning on the bottom of Huron:
my own home within my home.

A shimmer of color in the dark depths
of the water greets me
every morning when I wake. Sings

to me every evening when I drift to sleep.
A lullaby of hush and secret and light.

Lockdown Dive

It's all crazy making without my big sister,
and now, school closed, without a place to dive.
Or even talk. I touch
the amulet on its chain.

Aunt Claire says, *Try the lake.*
That's what it's for. Laughs. I pout
but wade out, shivery scared, the place
is that big. But then, the call of the dive

comes on, that longing for the falling
mixed with this thought: that
the lake is full of questions, same as me,
full of questions it wants answered.

Before I chicken out, I leap into it,
dive under. The cold shocks to my core,
but I kick down, hard, open my eyes
to murk and cloud, as far as I can hold

my breath into the chilled and silted light.
There's a secret, a portal in the rocks
where the lake rises in a colder current
and the water tastes like sulfur.

The Lost Sister

My own sister, my twin, the mermaid of Lake Michigan—
the sister with her blue/green hair—
is lost to me. We were born
from the same mother: the ancient
movement of ancient ice.
But now, we are apart.
A peninsula separates us
with its land, trees, rivers, and lakes.
This separation, this longing
that I feel every day,
is what I saw on the shore:
the woman and the girl,
the mermaid and her twin,
all bonded in their own sadness.

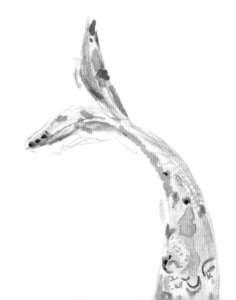

The Worst That Can Happen

. . . happens. The cell rings. My sister,
the bravest, strongest, most wild-haired
person in the world, my only sibling,

is sick, and there's no one who can go
to her. She can't hold the phone,
can't tell me to *straighten up*, to *fly right*.

I'm alone in Aunt Claire's town, our mom and dad
dead long ago. Here, few believe this word,
pandemic. I twist the charm at my throat.

My *sistersistersistersister*,
like the lap of waves on pebbles.
If she dies, there is no tomorrow,

only this shore with cold stones
who have such small, sharp voices.
I push them into my palms,

almost tearing open the lifeline,
the one she traced when she promised
to return. The stones mock me,

make a sinking song, like my thinking.
But when I dive, when waves cover me
over, the world cools down,

and in the wet chill, a presence, as though
the currents were kindred, as though
the lakes, too, were *sistered*.

I See the Girl

as if for the first time.
Not the young one on the shore,
hiding in her fear. But this

half-land, half-water creature
who is looking so hard
for her heart in the deep lake

where I live. How can I tell her?
I know that loneliness,
that heaviness, the sinking

like a stone. The never-never-ending doubt.
Like waves rushing, rushing,
against all sense of hope.

Only the morning can bring
light: a new day that begins

when the night ends. And
this new day is when
she's drawn to my home—

the cold current, the hidden life,
the algae that clings to rocks,
to my skin, hair, arms, scales.

This secret place of light
that surrounds me. Here,
she will find what she seeks: another

who has lost a sister.
Not because of a malady in the air
but because of the history of land.

A land that separates sister from sister,
lake of sunrise from lake of sunset.

The Taste

In my zoomed-out, zoomed-in science class,
I learn the name for that spot in the lake
where the darkness was not dark at all.

It's a sinkhole, opening to the farther deep,
to places even older than the oldest earth.
That's why the currents are sulfuric.

They rise from clefts way down
like a low fever from a deep lung,
and that's what I taste, bitter song

for my sister who has disappeared
as if in a sinkhole, not a hospital
where they promised she'd be safe.

But here, surrounding the dark center,
the algae that I long
to touch, to feel, blooms . . .

Oh, to have my sister, to touch her,
to hold her, to be a little sister again,
each thought a pull toward these waters,

each thought a wish for her to rise.
I hold my breath, hovering over
the lakescape until it's as though she,

or someone, is almost
there with me. Is that when the amulet
breaks from me and falls?

The Colors Falling

I imagine all the glowing colors

        of my lake gathered

    in one small stone—

          shimmering in half-light—

that stone falls from her neck

            and sinks/sinks/sinks

      down to where I weave the dawn.

Is it an old treasure,

      an ancient connection to a sister?

    I know about hers,

        but she does not know about mine.

And yet, this small glow fits in my hand

like a gift, a promise

to find what is lost.

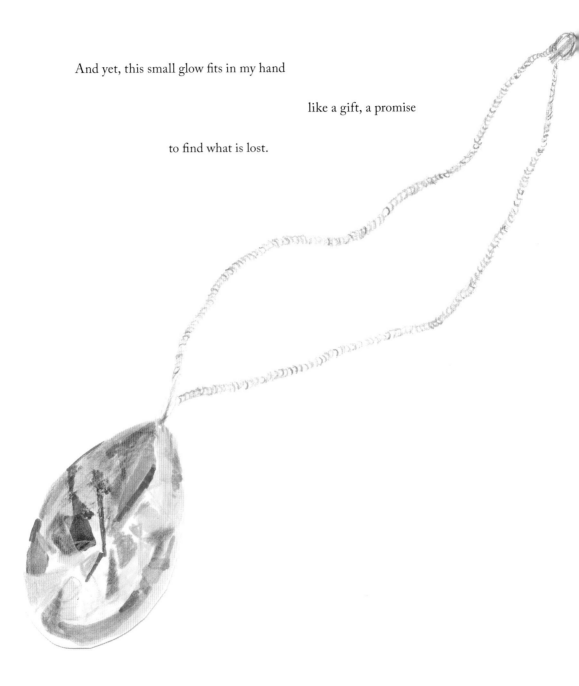

Kate's Whisper

When they bring Kate home,
I think she has recovered. I think
we will all be easy once again,

but when she comes, she cannot
speak too much, can barely walk,
cannot think quick the way she did.

I push her wheelchair down the path,
all the way to the rocks, then out
to the dock. Hope the air, the call

of waves will give her some hope—
that's what's gone, her wild hopes,
her dreams, her laugh. She falls asleep.

The name the doctors give this,
long hauling, long Covid,
long is long is now

days on end caring for her. I cool
her face and wrists. Kate whispers
her only question: *Where's the opal?*

The Mermaid Sings of Dreams

This radiance that has floated
into my open hand is filled
with dreams, but they are not
        mine, not mine.

Dreams of sorrow hovering
over land, over water. Dreams unfulfilled
are locked in this stone.
This stone that reflects
the sun and the moon
in its unblinking eye. Can I make
the dreams of sorrow
disappear with a song?
Can this gem's swirl of colored light
heal mind and body? Girl and sister?

       Light of the sunrise—

                    yellow ribbons of thin gold

       Light of the water—

                    blue glow reflecting the waves

       Light of the ice—

                    white ghost of silence

       Light of the earth—

                    green flashes from the shore

       Light of the wind—

                    transparent breath that sings

Light of the sky—

gray brilliance of clouds

Light of the sunset—

orange to rose to mauve dusk.

Warmth

She is not who she was.
　　　　She is not what she was.
She is always cold, does not walk, does
　　　　not look up, does not scold—

how I wish she would scold
　　　　me for any small forgotten thing,
Make your bed, pick up your clothes,
　　　　do the dishes. I could sass her back,

but now she's winded getting out of bed.
　　　　It makes me mad, hurts my heart.
I take to the waves, small escape between
　　　　long hours, dive as deep as I can

to the sinkhole's slime, cyanobacteria,
　　　　rainbowed otherworldly rift—
almost the colors of the amulet
　　　　magnified, made larger—a dream.

I will not find Kate's amulet;
　　　　I know that. But as I hover
above those fallen rainbows, a warmth rises
　　　　from the deeper dark,

as though someone has touched me,
　　　　　my arms, my face—but not.
Is it my Kate from the past?
　　　　　I can hold only a minute, but even

as my brief breath runs out,
　　　　　the place reminds me of what
I've lost, what I might find again
　　　　　if only she'd get better.

Her Lost Amulet, Her Waiting Hand

The girl cannot
see me but knows

I am here.
Her lost amulet

glows in the color
of my eyes

as I touch
her arm,

her hair.
And in that flash

of contact,
I place the stone of light

where it belongs—
in her waiting hand.

Miracle

I'm reaching into the deeps.
What I want, the softness

I don't believe in, not even
in these bacterial colonies

draped as blankets
over underwater rocks.

I'm reaching for the inside of—
call it pink, lavender, or a velvet

edge of stone-worn glass, that
gentling, that rounding off, not

the way they count the sick
now in thousands and beyond.

And how many are sisters?
And with my last seconds

of breath, a brush against skin,
barely there, my palm, then color,

and then I'm holding it,
the amulet, here in my hand.

Is this a miracle?

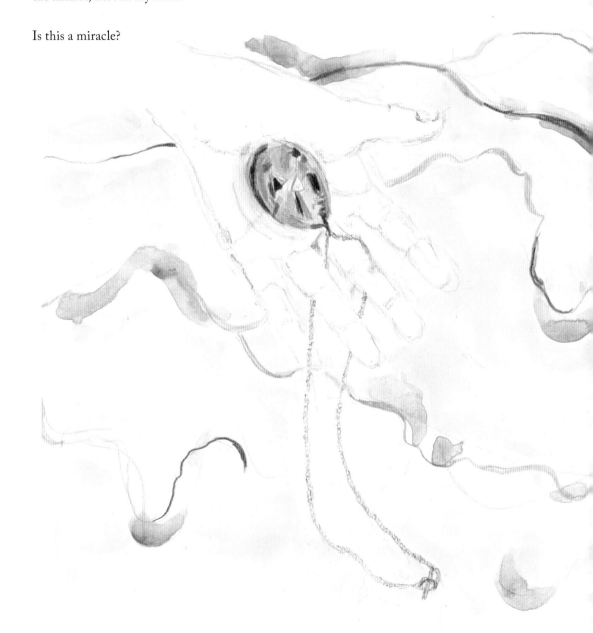

The Sunrise

A miracle—yes. Like the dawn,
the sun's rebirth every morning.
Its ball of flame that kisses me

awake, that starts the day,
that secretly calls our names.
All the murmurs of light and hope

and miracles. There, in your hand.
The stone reflects the rose-tinged sky
above the waters where I live.

I may hide in the depths
of colors buried at the bottom—
"velvet edge of stone-worn glass,"

you call it. But I know
my spirit lives in this lake's
flow and dance. My home,

the waves. My home, connected
to my sister—the aquamarine/
cold dazzle of her waters.

The sister who still calls
out to me. As the sun still
rises from my Huron,

the sun still sets in her Michigan.
Dawn to dusk. Lake to Lake.
The miracle continues. Every day,

every night. Now you,
who have felt me, help me
embrace my own miracle.

The sister I long for.

Trust

The docs say Kate's *a little better*, but
night sweats, brain fog, say she's not.
I hold our gem, sleep with it in hand.

Each day, I call a dozen numbers, not
one with a good answer. Except the one
scares me bad as too-cold water.

What does that do, vaccination?
It's coming, they say. *It helps some
long-haulers.* But what if it doesn't,

what if she turns worse, what if it plants
another virus in her soul, or some such
thing? I ask and ask. She looks out, face flat

as still water. I hold the opal to the sun
and ask again. Kate reaches for the rainbow
stone. That touch, that tie between us, sisters

like twin stars. I swear the stone's light warms
our hands. Kate looks up, awake, whispers,
Trust science. I remember the sinkhole,

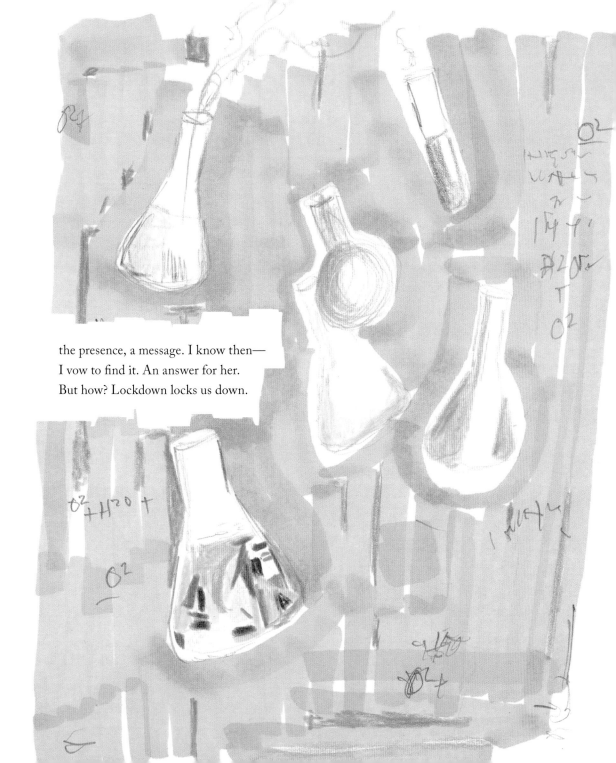

the presence, a message. I know then—
I vow to find it. An answer for her.
But how? Lockdown locks us down.

A New Hope

I can feel the sorrow stirring on the banks of my lake
and beyond—the illness, the death—but also
a new hope for the two sisters who are
as close as I was to my sister long ago.
            This hope, this other chance,
as people who breathe air
call it. Some believe and others do not
want to believe—in miracles, in the power
of the mind and its discoveries.
The earth sisters want to believe but need
a guide. My eyes glow with the light they hold.
I want to search the north waters

where my sister lives. Will they follow—
to find a healing for them, to find a sister for me?

Straits

I hear it first on the radio. It's coming to St. Ignace.
The first vaccines. I hold the opal in my hand,
watch the waves moving offshore, beyond the rocks.
The plan comes as if someone else thought of it.

Here it is: I earned my permit just before the virus,
learned to drive two-tracks long before that,
Aunt Claire riding shotgun. And our aunt never locks
her truck, and once Kate understands the plan,

she whispers one word, *Trouble*, grins a pale grin.
Trouble. But we are going, breaking out of lockdown,
heading north to the city where hope awaits,
where lake currents knot together,

where there is science to help us. We do it.
But when that truck, bald tires and all,
leans hard on that border road, I lose heart.
I'm scared. I send a thought to . . . the waters.

The light rises as if someone heard me,
an inner illumination, right out of that sinkhole.
It seems to lead us, it seems to guide,
it seems to know who we are, it seems here

that mystery and science collide.
As if another sister were with us, as if
the light linked us to Huron's waters?
We stop thinking, we follow.

The Straits of Mackinac link
the lakes, right? Huron and Michigan?
I forget the word *straits* goes two ways.
I forget the word also means plight, scrape,

even hot water, same as trouble.

True North

I follow the north with the sunrise:
that brilliant array of yellow/orange/rose/purple.
The colors weaving their light
like a fine, translucent stretch of cloth.

       I swim sleek and fast:
       silver in the water with my eyes
       glowing like small pieces of sunrise.
       I take my home with me—sky, horizon, water.

              I am the pale and quick flash:
              the faint light underwater. The islands I pass
              have always seen my comings and goings.
              I have been here many times before this long journey.

Gray rocks, driftwood, stunted white pines:
all the things I start to forget along this long coast
as I pass them—the blur of brown/green shore
leaves my memory and is swallowed by waves.

       I swim in those waves and watch:
       the two sisters traveling together
       on a long, thin ribbon of flat gray stone.
       As if the lake, my lake, made a path for them.

All the while, I swim/swim/swim:
the open water, the hope-giving water
that leads me to my true north—
the waters of my sister, the lake of sunsets.

And finally, I see it—the straits that connect:
lake to lake, the arc of the sky that joins
dawn to dusk. And the two earth sisters
wanting questions answered—to heal them.

None Left

We push that gas pedal hard, race
that old truck down Interstate 75,
push the speed limit across the bridge
we call Big Mac,
all the way to St. Ignace.

And then . . .
not one remains, not one dose
that might give her renewed
resistance—like an armor.
Not one left and no more to come.
Months or longer. Oh, they were kind,
sympathetic as can be. Hands empty.
They saw how she was. They said,
tired as they were—even I could see that—
Take care of each other, and I wanted

to throw something at them, tip over
the long tables, scatter their papers. Beg.
But Kate put her hands together
and bowed to them, and I saw
the nurses knew each other's work,
and then . . . what? . . . the respect that
passed like waves between them.
Their eyes were as sad as hers.
It silenced my words but not my heart.

Let Your Anger Dissolve . . .

like the waves, waves that can
lift you both up—you can rise,

rise from this long hour of anger
and deep frustration, the sinking frustration

of not getting what you so deserve,
what you want: oh, how I know

that feeling of helplessness, the feeling
of sinking so deep you cannot imagine

bottom, cannot see the light above you.
Listen, sisters, please. Sisters, listen to

me, to your hearts: you are both
alive, alive, not sunk into the earth

where darkness dwells but in the air that hovers
over water, water that binds sister to sister.

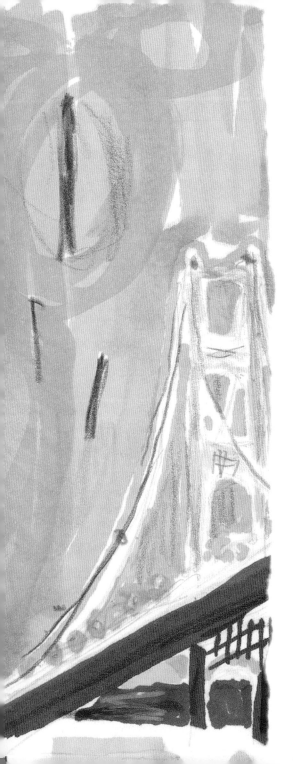

The Light

It's night when we hit the bridge again,
highway lamps glinting off struts
mocking my one-time, dimming hope.

There's no one, nothing but white lines
when right over the straits, truck sputters,
engine dies, and I coast to the side,

and there in the dark, I look at Kate,
and she shakes her head, teary-eyed.
She's so tired, she's a ragdoll.

I know I've done wrong,
made a mistake when she rouses,
Let's get out, right there, right then,

and we do. I open the doors, we climb
into the cold, to the green railing,
wind like birds' wings pushing us,

and we look down to where east meets west.
That light, as though a comet floated underwater,
hovers in the depths as if it, too, is stalled.

Look at that, I say. *She's waiting.*

Kate stares. *Who?* How do I answer,
tell her a creature from a sinkhole?
No. *The mermaid of Huron.* She smiles.

And like that, the world is poised,
watching too, even wind holding its breath
high in the middle of a too-high bridge.

Intertwined

After so much longing,
       I finally see it—
long stretch of arc
       bridging one piece of land
to another. And underneath it—
       the waters of two lakes
becoming one:
       my sister's sapphire eyes
shining to meet my iridescent gaze.
       The past, the present.
And our futures,
       forever intertwined.
We listen to our songs
       as we circle and merge,
circle and merge
       like the spectrum
of a prism that glows
       from brilliant
rose dawn
       to muted
blue dusk.

The currents of joy
around us ebb and flow,
        ebb and flow,
as we lake sisters
        dance and
embrace each other's
        light.

Gentle Weight

It happens like this—another light, glimmering
below, floating toward the one
we followed. Then—I am not sure—
the two join like soft hands,

dancing under the surface.
They spiral, silver water moths,
like you want the world to be,
that graceful, that . . . well, *together*

is the word that rises.
My bitterness floats out,
a dark gull
disappearing over waves.

Kate takes my hand, leans on my shoulder,
a gentle weight,
and we're almost as one,
almost like we once were,

except she's leaning on me, not me on her.
I take her hand, hold tight,
so she will know I will never let her go.
Not now, not ever.

The Long Journey Back

We begin the long journey back to our homes:
in the depths and on the shores of Huron,
the sunrise lake. The luminous lake
that abandons night and creates
the story of dawn, of morning, of a new
beginning every day. Dawn, you are named
as I am named: we are creatures born to catch
the sun and hold it. I cannot hold my sister

like you hold yours—hands tightly clasped—
but I know the life-giving embrace of her waters.
Water of sunrise, water of sunset, water of mermaids
and their dreams. And those dreams of sisters
bound to the land of gray rock and green field.
Bound to each other, closer now: like the shore to the water's edge.

Sisterdom

The years pass. Kate and I
learn to live another life, never far

from the waves, the waters,
the stony shores where we began.

The morning fogs, broken with light,
have softened our storms.

I hold Kate's hand, and she holds mine.
I dive Huron's sinkholes,

full of life still unknown,
and the scientist I am now

may yet unveil the link
between viruses and slime,

the sources of so much chemistry
and geologic history. The depths

even I cannot dive, the mats
of bacteria we have yet to name.

But most of all, mystery,
the heart of the planet, its making,

and my own; we may yet find
the secret of life's formation

where my mermaid lives.
Because even though I write

formulas, study oxygen levels,
I also know she is there—

I still feel her in the warm
rush of spirit rising from the depths.

The amulet glows with light
and hope. And sisterdom.

Contrapuntal: The Gift

All the way, I swim

        back toward a home,

back with the waters glowing,

        back to the morning shores

of prismed stone—the gift

        of waves and horizons

I gave to the girl

        where the dawn in a sister's eyes

has returned to me, light

        shines with the healing

of my sister's deep waters—

        rests in the palms of our hands,

flows in me forever

        and joins the currents of our lives.

Acknowledgments

The authors would like to thank Stephanie Williams, Marie Sweetman, Carrie Teefey, Rebecca Emanuelsen, and Wayne State University Press for their commitment in bringing our second Great Lakes mermaid story to readers and audiences alike. They also thank their husbands and families—especially Tony Foster, David Early, and Deborah Nemec—and their writing communities for their love and support.

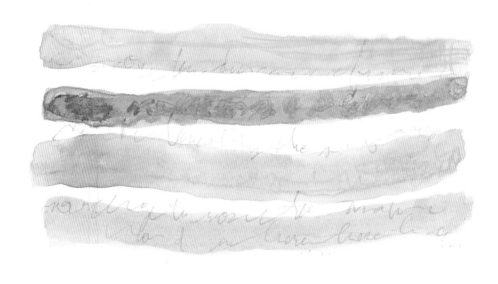

Further Reading

For more information, visit the following webpages:

ON THE SINKHOLES OF LAKE HURON

Microbial communities in Lake Huron sinkhole:

www.news.umich.edu/lake-huron-sinkhole-surprise-the-rise-of-oxygen-on-early-earth-linked-to-changing-planetary-rotation-rate

The Lake Huron Sinkhole project:

www.glerl.noaa.gov/res/projects/sinkhole

Lake Huron's sinkholes contain cyanobacteria:

www.greatlakesecho.org/2020/05/29/scientists-explore-mysterious-lake-huron-sinkholes

Water gain to Lake Huron through its sinkholes:

www.noaa.gov/stories/giant-sinkholes-are-adding-water-to-lake-huron-scientists-ask-how-much

ON FREE DIVING

Information on free diving:

www.deeperblue.com/what-is-freediving

No oxygen tanks in free diving:

www.thealpenanews.com/news/local-news/2021/08/thanks-but-no-tanks

Diving on a single breath:

www.michiganfreediving.com

ON LONG COVID

A review article on long Covid:

www.ncbi.nlm.nih.gov/pmc/articles/PMC8056514

Months of Covid symptoms:

https://health.ucdavis.edu/coronavirus/covid-19-information/
covid-19-long-haulers

Long Covid by another name:

www.webmd.com/lung/what-is-long-covid-pasc

ON THE ST. IGNACE VACCINE ROLLOUT

January 2021 Covid vaccine update from Mackinac Straits Health
System:

www.stignacenews.com/articles/covid-19-vaccine-update-from-
mackinac-straits-health-system

Covid vaccination events in the eastern Upper Peninsula:

www.stignacenews.com/articles/vaccine-effort-is-making-progress

Covid-19 vaccines available for all adults:

www.stignacenews.com/articles/covid-19-vaccines-now-available-
locally-to-all-adults-returning-snowbirds

About the Authors

LINDA NEMEC FOSTER is the founder of the Contemporary Writers Series at Aquinas College and has taught poetry workshops (K to adult level) throughout Michigan since 1980. She is the author of more than twelve collections of poetry and served as the inaugural Poet Laureate of Grand Rapids, Michigan (2003–05). Her poems have been widely praised and awarded nationally and abroad, including first prize in the Allen Ginsberg Poetry Awards, second prize in Ireland's Fish Publishing Poetry Prize, and Pulitzer Prize nominations for *Bone Country* and *The Blue Divide*.

Photo Credit: Dianne Carroll Burdick

ANNE-MARIE OOMEN teaches in the Solstice MFA program at Lasell University and at Interlochen College of Creative Arts and lives near Traverse City, Michigan. She has written eight books and is winner of the Association of Writers and Writing Program's Sue William Silverman Prize for Creative Nonfiction for *As Long as I Know You: The Mom Book*. She has written seven plays, and she is founding editor of *Dunes Review*, former president of Michigan Writers, and recipient of the Michigan Author Award for 2023–24.

About the Illustrator

MERIDITH RIDL is an artist and art teacher with a BA in studio art from the College of Wooster and an MFA from the University of Michigan. Much of her painting and drawing work explores gestures that might suggest tenderness, humor, gentleness, loneliness—arrangements that might have a wobble, or that "aren't quite right." Her work ranges from meditative, delicate, and quiet to more tipsy and quirky. Meridith lives in West Michigan where she often wanders the woods and lakeshore. Her work is represented by LaFontsee Galleries in Grand Rapids, Michigan.